Is Caroline Pearce a noodle nabber?

"Where's Caroline?" Lila asked, looking around the playground. I glanced around too but didn't see her.

Lila thumped her finger on her chin. "You know what, Elizabeth? I saw Caroline leave lunch early. Maybe she snuck back to the room and tore the macaroni off your project."

Jessica's mouth dropped open. "Maybe! She *was* awfully jealous."

I gasped. Caroline would never do something *that* sneaky. Would she?

Bantam Books in the SWEET VALLEY KIDS series

THE MACARONI MESS

Written by
Molly Mia Stewart

Created by
FRANCINE PASCAL

Illustrated by
Marcy Ramsey

BANTAM BOOKS
NEW YORK · TORONTO · LONDON · SYDNEY · AUCKLAND

RL 2, 005-008

THE MACARONI MESS
A Bantam Book / September 1997

*Sweet Valley High® and Sweet Valley Kids® are
registered trademarks of Francine Pascal.*

Conceived by Francine Pascal.

*Produced by Daniel Weiss Associates, Inc.
33 West 17th Street
New York, NY 10011.*

Cover art by Wayne Alfano.

*All rights reserved.
Copyright © 1997 by Francine Pascal.
Cover art and interior illustrations copyright © 1997 by
Daniel Weiss Associates, Inc.
No part of this book may be reproduced or transmitted
in any form or by any means, electronic or mechanical,
including photocopying, recording, or by any information
storage and retrieval system, without permission in
writing from the publisher.
For information address: Bantam Books.*

*If you purchased this book without a cover, you should be aware
that this book is stolen property. It was reported as "unsold and
destroyed" to the publisher and neither the author nor the publisher has
received any payment for this "stripped book."*

ISBN: 0-553-48339-0

Published simultaneously in the United States and Canada

*Bantam Books are published by Bantam Books, a division of Bantam
Doubleday Dell Publishing Group, Inc. Its trademark, consisting of the
words "Bantam Books" and the portrayal of a rooster, is Registered in the
U.S. Patent and Trademark Office and in other countries. Marca
Registrada. Bantam Books, 1540 Broadway, New York, New York 10036.*

PRINTED IN THE UNITED STATES OF AMERICA

OPM   0 9 8 7 6 5 4 3 2 1

To James Ryan

CHAPTER 1
Field Trip Fun

"That was an awesome field trip, Elizabeth," said my twin sister, Jessica, as we got into the bus and took our seats. We had just finished going through the Sweet Valley Art Museum and were heading back to school.

I nodded excitedly. "I know! Which part did you like better? Looking at paintings in the museum? Or watching all the different artists working at the arts and crafts fair?"

"Watching the artists, definitely," Jessica replied. "Seeing people make art is so much more fun than looking at paintings on a wall."

"But lots of the paintings in the museum were *so* nice—and *so* famous—and *so* expensive," Lila Fowler added. She was the richest girl in Sweet Valley. "I liked the one by Picasso. My daddy has one just like it."

Charlie Cashman rolled his eyes. "I thought some of the art was kind of dumb. Remember that painting of toilet paper?"

"Yeah!" Jerry McAllister replied. "Who cares about that? I see toilet paper every time I go into a bathroom."

Jessica and I laughed. Even though Jerry acted like a bully sometimes, he could still be really funny. But Charlie was usually just plain mean.

Charlie poked Jerry in the ribs. "The picture with the mirror in it reminded me of the twins," Charlie said.

"What do you mean?" Jerry asked.

"The reflection in the mirror made it look like there were two of the exact same thing," Charlie explained, a nasty smile on his face. "Remember what it was?"

"I remember," I said, frowning. "It was a *monkey!*"

Charlie doubled over with laughter. "That's *especially* why it reminded me of *you* two." He scratched his armpits and made monkey noises.

"Takes one to know one," Jessica said, tossing her hair.

I should probably introduce myself. I'm Elizabeth Wakefield. My sister, Jessica, and I are special because we're the only twins at Sweet Valley Elementary. We're in second grade, and we look totally alike. We have long blond hair and blue-green eyes and a dimple in our left cheek. We wear name bracelets to school so the other kids can tell us apart. But sometimes it's fun to switch and fool people. We've even tricked our mom and dad and our big brother, Steven.

We don't always dress alike. My favorite color is blue, and Jessica's is pink. I like to wear my hair in a

4

ponytail, but Jessica likes to wear hers down. When we want to mix people up, we each wear the other's favorite color, and she wears her hair in a ponytail like me.

Even though we're twins, we're different in lots of ways. I like to play soccer and ride horses. I don't mind getting dirty when I play outside. That's part of the fun. But Jessica hates getting her clothes dirty, and she doesn't like to play sports. She's the best rope jumper in class, though.

I love school, and I don't mind doing homework. But Jessica hates school. Our mom has to make sure she does her work. During class Jessica passes notes to her friends when our teacher, Mr. Crane, is talking. Her best friends, besides me of course, are Ellen Riteman and Lila. Mine are

Todd Wilkins and Amy Sutton. Jessica would *never* have a boy for a best friend. She thinks boys are gross.

One boy she does like is our teacher, Mr. Crane. He's really funny and nice and wears cool clothes. Today, for our art field trip, he wore a shirt that looked like it had paint splashes on it and a bright blue tie. Mr. Crane loves animals too. He brings a different animal to class every week.

As our bus pulled up in front of Sweet Valley Elementary, Mr. Crane stood up and announced, "Get ready, kids. I have two big surprises waiting for you when we get back to room two-oh-three."

Jessica and I looked at each other and smiled. What would the surprises be?

CHAPTER 2

Meeting Petey

"OK, everyone, listen up," Mr. Crane said as we all took our seats in room 203. He whistled to get our attention. Another loud whistling sound followed it like an echo—but Mr. Crane had only whistled once!

"Hey, where'd that other whistle come from?" Todd asked.

Suddenly Mr. Crane uncovered a huge birdcage in the corner of the room. A bright yellow-and-green parrot hopped on the wooden swing, flapped his wings, and whistled again. We all laughed.

"This is Petey," Mr. Crane announced.

"Hi, Petey!" we all shouted.

"Hi, Petey! Hi, Petey!" the parrot repeated. We laughed again.

Mr. Crane sat on his desk. "You'll have plenty of time to get to know Petey. But for now let's share what we liked best about our field trip today."

A few people groaned. "Is this the other surprise?" Ricky Capaldo asked.

"No," Mr. Crane answered. "But it will help you prepare for it."

"My favorite part was snack time," Tom McKay said. "Is the surprise a snack?"

"Sorry, it's not." Mr. Crane smiled.

"Jessica, what did you like best?"

"I liked watching that lady make doll clothes at the art fair," Jessica said. "They were so pretty."

"I liked the painting of the knight on a horse," Andy Franklin spoke up. "It was really realistic."

"I liked watching the glass-blower," Ken Matthews offered. "That guy's got a lot of hot air."

"I liked the big painting that had all the gooshy paint splotches on it," Winston Egbert said. "It looked like your shirt, Mr. Crane. I want to paint a picture just like it."

Mr. Crane snapped his fingers. "Good idea, Winston. In fact, that's my other surprise—we're going to have our own art show right here in room two-oh-three. And your parents will all be invited!"

Wow—our very own art show! Everyone cheered. I was so excited, my heart felt like a Ping-Pong ball bouncing up and down.

"Can I use paint and an easel like a real artist?" Winston asked.

"Sure," Mr. Crane said. "You can use anything you want. You can make pictures out of beans or paint or work with papier-mâché or clay. When you use your imagination, anything is possible."

"I want to use clay," Amy said.

"Me too," Eva Simpson agreed.

"I want to make a papier-mâché snake," Charlie announced.

"Gross!" Lila shouted.

"That's why I want to make it," Charlie sneered. "Because you girls are afraid of snakes."

"No, I didn't mean snakes, Charlie."

Lila stuck out her tongue and showed off her perfectly polished fingernails. "I hate papier-mâché even more. That paste gets my hands all messy."

Mr. Crane clapped to get our attention. "How would you kids like to take the paints, easels, crayons, and paper outside and make art for the rest of the day?"

"All right!" Tom shouted.

"That'll be fun!" I said.

"Can we take Petey outside with us?" Eva asked.

"Sure," Mr. Crane replied with a smile.

As we loaded the art supplies onto the rolling cart, Lila turned up her nose at the old paintbrushes and worn-down crayons. "I wish we had nicer, newer art stuff," she said snobbily. "Then I could paint a picture that would be so perfect, it would sell for a million dollars."

"And I could paint a big green fire-breathing dragon that'd be so real, it would eat you," Jerry said. All the boys laughed, but Lila held her head up high and ignored them.

I twirled the end of my ponytail around my finger and wondered what I would make for the art show. I wanted it to be something really special: an Elizabeth Wakefield original. But what would it be?

CHAPTER 3
Todd's Crazy Cartoons

"I feel like a real artist," Winston said as he spattered paint onto a big piece of poster board. He danced around his easel while he worked.

"Me too," I agreed. I was painting big green swirls and little green lines. I hadn't really thought about what I wanted to paint, but the green lines looked like vines in a jungle.

Petey whistled.

I giggled. "I painted the perfect place for you, didn't I, Petey?"

Petey whistled again.

"Hey, that's pretty." Jessica hugged me. "I think yours is the best, Lizzie."

"You're just saying that 'cause she's your twin," Caroline Pearce whined.

"That's not true," Jessica said, crossing her arms. "Hers *is* the best." She took a step backward. Todd was sitting on the grass behind her, drawing in a sketch pad. She tripped on Todd's foot and screamed. Todd's pad flew into the air and landed with its pages open, flapping in the wind.

Winston ran over to look. "Hey, check out Todd's pictures."

Todd scrambled to get his pad. "No, you guys. I'm saving those for the art show."

Charlie held up the pad for everyone to see. On the first page Todd had drawn a picture of Mr. Crane wearing one of his wild-looking shirts. Petey was sitting on Mr. Crane's shoulder and nibbling on his curly hair.

"That's really good," Eva said.

"Yeah. It looks just like Mr. Crane," Jim Sturbridge agreed.

Then Charlie flipped the page to a drawing of Lila. You could tell it was supposed to be her because her nose was long and pointy and was stuck up in the air so high, it almost reached the sun. Everyone laughed except Lila, of course. She gave Todd a nasty look.

The next drawing was of Lois Waller. Lois always wears a huge purple sweater, so Todd had drawn it to look like a big bunch of purple grapes with Lois's little head on top.

"Perfect!" Jerry said. But Lois looked down and stared at her dirty sneakers.

"Stop, you guys," Todd said, trying to get the pad back.

"Hey, did you draw one of me?" Jerry flipped the page and found a drawing of Andy. Andy's glasses were drawn so big, he looked like a space alien. Some of the kids hooted with laughter, but Andy's face turned as red as a cherry.

The next drawing was of a girl who had a long tail and a mouth as big as her whole head.

"That's Caroline!" Winston shouted.

"Nuh-uh!" Caroline cried.

"Winston's right," Ellen said. "You have a tail because you're such a tattletale. Get it? Tail? Tale?"

Caroline stomped away. "I'm going to tell on you, Todd," she yelled over her shoulder.

We all laughed. But when Jerry turned the next page, my stomach did a somersault.

It was a drawing of *me!*

It had to be, since it was of a girl who had a long blond ponytail and was kicking a soccer ball. But Todd had drawn my legs really long, and my feet were *huge!*

"My feet aren't *that* big," I complained. "Are they?"

"No," Jessica said. "It's just a bad drawing."

"It's a cartoon," Todd said, looking upset. "It's supposed to be funny."

"Well, it's *not!*" I snapped, staring at him hard. I read something once about a guy who could burn holes through people with his eyes, so I tried to do that. But then the dismissal bell rang, and I didn't get to see if it worked.

"Hey, Bigfoot," Charlie teased me. "Think you can make it home without tripping?"

I gritted my teeth until I got back to room 203. Everyone grabbed their book bags and jackets while Caroline told Mr. Crane how mean Todd's drawings were.

"I'm sure Todd didn't mean to hurt your feelings," Mr. Crane said. "Todd's drawings are called caricatures."

"Carry-what?" Winston asked.

"Care-i-kuh-chures," Mr. Crane

explained. "They're kind of like cartoons. That's how Todd likes to express himself through art."

"Well, I feel like expressing *my*self through punching him in the nose," Lila whispered.

For once I actually agreed with Lila. The day had started off fun and gone downhill fast, like a bad roller-coaster ride. And if Todd kept drawing caricatures, everyone who came to the art show would see me looking like Bigfoot!

CHAPTER 4

Art Smarts

"Lizzie, are you awake?" Jessica whispered to me that night after we had gone to bed.

"Yes," I whispered back, hugging my stuffed koala bear.

"What are you going to make for your art project?"

"I don't know yet."

"I know what I'm going to make," Jessica said. "A princess's crown. I thought of it during recess when I was playing Princess with Lila."

"That's perfect for you, Jess." I could tell Jessica was smiling, so I smiled too. That's one neat thing about being a twin. Sometimes we know what the other one is thinking and feeling deep down inside.

When Jessica's breathing got quiet, I knew she'd fallen asleep. But I wasn't sleepy. All I could think about was what I would make for my project. Suddenly I remembered how Charlie had teased me and said my project should be a pair of giant feet made out of clay.

"Maybe you should make a *brain* out of clay, Charlie, since you don't have one," Jessica had said. That's another great thing about being a twin. You always have someone to stand up for you.

I stared at the shadows on the

ceiling while I tried to think of an idea.

Watercolors? Chicken-wire sculpture? Sewing? Stenciling? Sticker art? Balloon art? Sand art?

My mind was whirling with ideas, but none of them seemed right.

Papier-mâché? Paper collage? Puppet making?

My eyelids got heavy, but I blinked and tried to stay awake. *A doll? Basket weaving?*

I must have finally fallen asleep because the next thing I knew, it was time to get ready for school. All night I had dreamed of building a tower out of toothpicks to hold my eyelids open.

When we walked into room 203, Lila was showing off a huge, new, expensive-looking art kit.

"My mom sent it to me from Paris," Lila bragged. "Look, these are calligraphy pens. And these are charcoal sticks."

"Wow!" Jessica exclaimed.

"This is the neatest art kit I've ever seen!" Ellen cried.

"I got an art kit for my last birthday," Sandy Ferris said, touching one of the beautiful new paint-brushes. "But it only had markers and crayons."

"No one can use this kit but me and Jessica." Lila snapped the kit shut and smiled. "I'm going to make the best project in the show."

We all ignored her.

"Hey, Elizabeth, are you and Jessica going to make twin projects?" Ellen asked.

"No," we answered at the same time. Everyone laughed.

Mr. Crane walked in and set a bunch of bags on the floor. They had Grant's Art Supplies printed on the side.

"Mr. Crane!" Jessica called. "Come look at Lila's art kit!"

Lila opened the box, and Mr. Crane peeked inside. "Wow, Lila. That looks really professional."

"It is," Lila said. "My mom sent it from Paris."

I gritted my teeth. Jessica hardly ever got tired of Lila's bragging, but I did. A *lot*.

Jerry looked at Petey and wiggled his eyebrows. "I'm going to paint with bird feathers."

Everyone looked at Petey, then at Jerry. "You're not using Petey's feathers," I said.

"No way," Amy said.

"No way! No way!" Petey flapped his wings.

Amy stood in front of Petey's cage, and Ellen and Eva joined her. They made a circle around Petey, guarding him.

"I wasn't going to." Jerry laughed. "I'm going to find bird feathers in the park."

"Good for you," Mr. Crane said.

"I'm going to use my rock collection in my project," Jim said.

Caroline grinned. "I've got the best idea. But it's a secret."

My jaw dropped open. Caroline

was a blabbermouth. She didn't even know how to keep a secret!

Now pretty much everyone knew what to make but me. What was I going to do? My heart pounded the same way it always did right before I rode horses. Then I had an idea. I could make a picture of the pony I liked to ride! But how could I make it really special?

I found out how that night. Because when I got home, my mom had just been to the grocery store. There, on the counter, was a box of macaroni noodles.

That was it! I could paint my pony and glue macaroni all over it. I asked my mom if it was OK. She gave me the box and said, "Your project sounds wonderful, Elizabeth."

Hurray! I finally had come up with the perfect project—something that no one else would do. It would truly be an Elizabeth Wakefield original.

CHAPTER 5
The Macaroni Pony

"What are you making, Elizabeth?" Eva asked me the next morning before attendance.

I smiled, remembering the box of macaroni hidden in my backpack. "It's a secret."

"Come on, tell us," Todd begged.

I shook my head. "You'll see this afternoon."

Mr. Crane came in and told us that we could work on our art projects after lunch. From then on the clock ticked slower than a turtle walking across the road. When lunchtime finally came, I wolfed down my macaroni and cheese.

"What's your secret?" Ellen asked. "Are you making sponge pictures?"

I shook my head.

"A button bear?" Eva asked.

"You'll see." I giggled and looked down at my macaroni and cheese. Nobody had guessed my secret—and we were having it for lunch!

After lunch Mr. Crane put out paint, construction paper, glue sticks, glitter, and all kinds of drawing and painting stuff. Lots of the other kids in class had brought things from home too.

"Come on, Jess." Lila grabbed Jessica's hand. "Let's work with my art kit." They huddled in the corner and pulled out charcoal sticks and chalk and some shiny paper.

Amy had brought in her one-eyed teddy bear and some felt. "Look, Elizabeth. I'm going to make Mr. Golly a special blanket to keep him warm."

"That's super," I said, feeling a little jealous. It was a great idea. Why didn't I think of that?

"I'll glue buttons and fringe on it, and it'll be perfect." Amy tried to pin the fringe in place, but she stuck her finger. "Ouch!"

"Maybe Mr. Crane should help you," I told her. I was probably better off not making a blanket. It could get dangerous!

"Look what Andy brought in," Julie Porter whispered.

I glanced at Andy and covered my mouth. "Dead bugs?"

Julie nodded and made a face. "He's making a dead bug collage."

I shivered and got to work. Amy had gotten Mr. Crane to help pin the fringe around the edges of her blanket. While she fastened it with glue, I sketched my pony on a big sheet of paper very carefully. I decided to use brown paint for his body and yellow for his mane and tail.

Kisho Murasaki sat nearby. He was folding paper into different animal shapes. Charlie was dropping marbles in paint, then putting them in a box. He would tilt the box and move it around so the marbles rolled from side to side on his paper and made designs.

"What are you making, Eva?" I asked.

Eva shaped small pieces of white

clay into circles. "Refrigerator magnets." She used a small cookie cutter and cut out a cat shape. "When they dry, I'm going to paint them. Then I'll glue magnets on the back. My mom taught me how."

"Cool," Amy said.

Andy dangled one of his dead bugs in front of Amy's face. She squealed and stuck her finger with a pin again. "Ouch! Look what you made me do." She glared at Andy.

I splashed more brown paint on my paper and noticed Jessica giggling. She was making a crown out of construction paper and glitter. Silver glitter sparkled in her hair, and little dots of it were stuck to the tip of her nose.

I finished painting my pony. While

it dried, I looked at the other kids' projects. Jerry had dipped feathers in different colors of paint, then brushed them across his paper. Tom had glued together a bunch of wooden blocks in the shape of a pyramid. Julie had made a bunny out of cotton balls. Sandy had poured different colors of sand into a glass to make sand art. Ricky had glued toothpicks together to make a box.

"It's a garage for my toy cars," Ricky explained.

Lois took off her shoes.

Winston pinched his nose. "P.U."

Lois frowned. "I'm going to make feet prints."

Mr. Crane helped Lois by steadying her as she stepped into a tray of purple paint.

"It's cold," Lois squealed. She

stepped from the paint tub and pressed her foot on the paper.

"That should be you, Bigfoot," Charlie yelled at me. I glared at Charlie, then Todd. Todd gave me a sad look. Why was he sad? It was his fault everyone was teasing me.

When no one was looking, I got my box of macaroni and glued the dried pieces on my pony. Everyone was so busy, they didn't even notice my secret yet.

Caroline slammed her hand on the table. "This isn't working!" she cried.

"What are you making?" I asked her.

Caroline's lip trembled. "It's a potato head doll."

I looked at the lopsided potato but didn't say anything. I had to admit it was kind of messy. OK, *really* messy.

"Your potato must be sick," Charlie teased.

Caroline's face turned red. "It's going to be really good when I fin-ish!"

Suddenly I heard my name being called. "Elizabeth!" Amy shouted. "Your pony is so cool! I'd never think of using macaroni."

"I love it, Lizzie." Jessica hugged me.

Charlie peered over my shoulder. Jim and Jerry and Ricky stood beside him. Even Todd came over. "Awesome," he said.

"I wish I'd thought of that," Ricky said.

"What are you calling it?" Lois asked.

"I know!" Winston jumped up and

down. "Call it the macaroni pony."

"Macaroni pony, macaroni pony," Petey echoed.

Amy giggled. "Even Petey likes it."

"I think it's the best project in the class," Ellen said.

My heart went thumpity-thumpity-thump. Everyone liked my macaroni pony! Now maybe everyone would forget about Todd's drawing of me with gigantic elephant feet.

CHAPTER 6

Caroline Gets Jealous

"Hey, Winston, what is that?" Ricky asked.

Winston grinned. He'd painted a whole bunch of pictures and hung them on a clothesline to dry. Dots of red paint were smeared on his chin, and he had a squiggly line of yellow paint on his eyebrow. "You mean you can't tell?"

The class gathered around and stared at the pictures. Everyone except Caroline. She was trying to stick some buttons on her potato head doll for eyes, but they kept falling off.

I squinted at Winston's art, but it didn't look like anything but shapes and colors. Jim turned his head sideways. Andy cleaned his glasses, then put them on again. Still no one answered.

"We give up," Jim said.

Winston pointed to the one covered with paint blobs. "It's a rainstorm."

"But rain isn't yellow," Amy said.

40

"Or orange and purple," Charlie said.

"And what's this one?" Ricky pointed to a picture of a bunch of squares with black dots in the middle.

"It's a quilt," Eva said.

Winston shook his head. "That's a dog locked in a cage."

Charlie and Jerry got closer to the picture. "I don't see a dog," Charlie said.

"Me neither," Jerry said. "It looks like a checkerboard to me."

I leaned forward, trying to figure out how a dot could be a dog.

"I know what this one is." Lila pointed to a group of white smudgy spots on a green background. "It's a cloudy sky."

Winston shook his head again. "Uh-uh. That's a bunny rabbit hopping in the grass."

"That can't be a rabbit," Jim said.

"It is too," Winston said. "I should know. I painted it."

"If that's a bunny rabbit, where're its ears?" Ellen asked.

"And its tail and eyes?" Julie added.

Mr. Crane came over and smiled. "Winston's paintings are *abstract*," he said while Winston puffed out his chest proudly. "We saw abstract art at the museum, remember? Those paintings looked like nothing more than colors and shapes, but they mean much more."

"Well, it still looks like clouds to me," Lila insisted.

"And that one still looks like a quilt," Eva said.

"And rain is clear, not yellow," Charlie added.

"You're nuts." Ricky twirled his

42

finger in circles next to his head. "Those pictures look like a monkey painted them."

Winston drew a fat black line across the paper. "That's the way you guys think. No imagination."

"Well, Elizabeth has imagination," Amy said. "Her *Macaroni Pony* is the best!"

I smiled, but then I caught Caroline glaring at me. Glue was running down the side of her potato. She tried to wrap a small scrap of material around it to make a hat, but it kept slipping and falling off.

Charlie laughed. "I think Caroline's potato is pretty, uh, *abstract.*"

Caroline's cheeks turned crimson. "I don't care what you think, Charlie." She stuck two toothpicks in the potato's sides for arms. Her eyes filled with tears.

I hurried over. "Maybe I can help you?"

Caroline chewed her bottom lip. "No," she said. "Just because everyone likes yours doesn't mean I need you to do mine." She threw down her materials. "I don't care about this stupid art show anyway." Caroline burst into tears and ran from the room.

Mr. Crane rushed over. "What happened?"

"Caroline was having trouble with her project," Amy said.

Mr. Crane looked concerned. "Amy, would you check and see if she's in the girls' room, please?"

"OK," Amy said.

"Thank you," Mr. Crane said. "Let me know if she's not, and I'll go look for her. The rest of you, please finish up for today."

Jessica put her arm around me. "I like your pony. Don't worry about what Caroline said. She's just jealous."

"Thanks, Jess." I looked at my macaroni pony and felt all tingly with pride. But then I saw Caroline's sad-looking potato lying on the floor, and I couldn't help but feel bad for her.

CHAPTER 7

The Macaroni Mess

"Let's make invitations for your parents for the art show," Mr. Crane announced the next morning as he passed out construction paper. "Decorate the front of your invitation any way you want."

"This will be fun!" Winston shouted. I wondered what kind of weirdo painting he was going to put on his.

Mr. Crane pulled a bag of sticky tack from his desk. "While you're working on your invitations, I'll come around and pick people to hang up their projects."

I looked at Todd and saw his sketch pad sticking out of his desk. Todd stared at me, then started drawing. I wished Mr. Crane would change his mind about Todd's pictures. They made our class look like a bunch of goofballs.

"Good job," Mr. Crane said to Winston as he put up five of his paintings.

"Good job, good job," Petey repeated.

"That bird doesn't know much about art," Jim said.

"Maybe he needs glasses," Andy suggested.

Everyone chuckled. When Mr. Crane called Caroline's name, she placed a soft white doll on one of the display tables.

"Wow, Caroline, you must have worked hard on that," Mr. Crane said.

"It's beautiful," Jessica said. "Did you make it?"

"Of course," Caroline answered in a snippy voice.

"I wish you'd teach me how to make a doll like that," Eva said.

"Me too," Ellen agreed.

I stared at the white handkerchief dress and the stitches on the face. They were really good. But then I remembered the time we'd sewn pillows in class. Caroline's stitches had been big and sloppy like mine.

Had Caroline really made the doll by herself?

"Lila?" Mr. Crane called.

Lila shook her head. "I'm not finished with mine."

"The show's tomorrow, Lila," Mr. Crane said. "Will you be finished by then?"

"I don't know." Lila shrugged and put on an I-don't-care face. "I may not be in the art show after all."

Mr. Crane gave her a puzzled look, then asked Jerry to come up.

"What's wrong with Lila?" I whispered to Jessica. "What is she making?"

Jessica leaned over. "She doesn't know how to use some of that stuff in her fancy kit. She's too embarrassed to admit it after bragging so much."

"Jessica and Elizabeth, come hang up your art," Mr. Crane said.

I jumped up, and Jessica followed. "I love your crown," I told Jessica.

"And your pony is beautiful," Jessica said.

She put her crown in the middle of the table beside Caroline's doll and Tom's wood-block pyramid and Ken's tin-can sculpture. "I'm not putting it anywhere near Andy's bugs," Jessica whispered.

I hung my macaroni pony beside Amy's blanket for Mr. Golly. The macaroni looked great. I was so proud!

"Lunchtime," Mr. Crane announced.

Charlie rubbed his stomach. "Your pony made me hungry."

"Why don't you eat some of Andy's bugs?" Todd suggested.

I laughed and noticed Todd watching me. But he looked away. When we got to the lunchroom, he sat by Ken.

"I thought of something easy for you to make," Jessica told Lila. Lila smiled, and they whispered all through lunch.

Winston took out his usual peanut butter and mayonnaise sandwich. He had three bananas too. He stacked them up in front of him. "Look, it's a sculpture. Maybe I should enter this in the show." But the tower leaned over, and the bananas toppled onto the floor.

I got up to pick them up, but my foot slipped. I reached for the table, but it was no use. My fingers barely touched the edge. My feet flew out from under me. I landed on the floor, right on top of Winston's bananas. Winston laughed.

"You banana brain!" I yelled. "Don't laugh at me. I was trying to help you."

"If I'm the banana brain, then how come you're the one with bananas all over you?" Winston said.

I brushed off my seat. Yuck! There was slimy, squishy banana gunk all over my jeans.

I trudged back to room 203 and got cleaned up. While I was looking at the art on display, my stomach jumped up into my throat. My macaroni pony was a mess! Almost all the macaroni pieces were gone. They had been torn off the paper, and bits were broken and scattered all over the floor like someone had stomped on them. There were lots of holes from where the macaroni had been torn off, and the whole thing had been ripped almost in half!

"Oh, no!" I cried just when the rest of the class started coming back from lunch.

Jessica ran over. "Elizabeth, what happened?"

"My macaroni pony's ruined. What am I going to do?"

Mr. Crane patted my shoulder. "It'll be all right, Elizabeth."

I wiped the tears from my eyes. It wasn't going to be all right. Tomorrow was the art show. Dad was taking off work, and Mom was missing one of her decorating classes. They'd see how awful my macaroni pony looked. And they'd see Todd's drawing of me with elephant feet too!

CHAPTER 8
Taking Sides

"You can paint a new pony when we go inside," Jessica said. She was trying to cheer me up during recess. "Or you can use my glitter and make a crown. We'll have twin projects."

I didn't want to hurt Jessica's feelings, but I didn't want a twin project. Then everyone would think I'd copied Jessica. I wanted my art to be an Elizabeth Wakefield original. "Thanks, Jess, but I want my pony."

"Where's Caroline?" Lila asked,

looking around the playground. I glanced around too but didn't see her.

Lila thumped her finger on her chin. "You know what, Elizabeth? I saw Caroline leave lunch early. Maybe she snuck back to the room and tore the macaroni off your project."

Jessica's mouth dropped open. "Maybe! She *was* awfully jealous."

I gasped. Caroline would never do something *that* sneaky. Would she?

"Time to line up," Mrs. Grimley announced. We formed a line.

"Caroline's not here," Lila said. "She never came out. She's guilty!"

I shrugged and didn't say anything. But when we walked back to class, I couldn't believe what I saw. Caroline was in the room all by herself. And she was standing near my project!

I put my hands on my hips. "You messed up my pony, didn't you, Caroline?"

Caroline shook her head, her hair bouncing around her shoulders. "I did not!"

"You did too."

"That's not true," Caroline shouted. Her eyes grew big and wild.

"It is too." I blinked back tears.

Jessica and some of the other kids ran over. "What is it, Elizabeth?" Jessica asked.

I pointed at Caroline. "Caroline tore up my project because she wanted hers to be the best."

"Caroline!" Jessica shouted.

"I did not!" Caroline yelled. "Elizabeth's mad 'cause her picture's ruined, and she wants to blame me because I've got a better project now."

"Well, my pony was fine when I put it up!" I shouted.

"Maybe the glue wasn't dry!" Caroline screamed.

"It was so!" My voice was shaking. "You messed it up!"

"You were the only one in here, Caroline," Lila said.

Lois stood beside Caroline. "But Caroline said she didn't do it."

Ellen moved to my side. "Elizabeth doesn't lie."

Sandy jumped over beside Lois.

"Well, neither does Caroline."

Amy stood on my other side. "We all heard Caroline yelling at Elizabeth yesterday. She was jealous."

"What's there to be jealous about?" Julie asked, taking Caroline's side.

Todd stepped over to my side. Pretty soon the other boys joined in. Everybody was shouting at everyone else.

"Elizabeth doesn't lie!"

"Neither does Caroline!"

A loud whistle broke into the noise. Everyone stopped shouting and looked at Charlie. Charlie grinned and drew a pretend line on the floor with his shoe. "We should ask Mr. Crane to divide the room in half—the Elizabeth side and the Caroline side."

Mr. Crane came in with a bunch of

papers. "What's all this noise about?"

Everyone dashed to their seats. "Nothing," I said. No one else said anything either. When I looked at my messed-up picture, I wanted to yell. But I didn't think it would be right to tell on Caroline to Mr. Crane—not when I didn't know for sure if she had messed up my macaroni pony.

After we worked on spelling and math, Mr. Crane let us work on our art projects again. Jessica was helping Lila make a magic wand out of a cardboard tube, tinfoil, and glitter. I was all alone, trying to glue broken pieces of macaroni back on my painting, when Todd came and sat down next to me.

"I thought you'd think the picture of you was funny," Todd said.

"Well, I didn't. Everyone laughed at me."

"They were laughing at the drawing," Todd said. "That's what cartoons make people do. But the only reason I drew the big feet was because you can run so fast."

"What?" I looked up at him. He was staring out the window. "Yeah, you're the best. You always beat me when we race."

I hadn't thought about that.

"And you're great at soccer." Todd's cheeks turned pink.

"That's why you drew me with big feet?"

"Well, yeah. Why'd you think I did it?"

"I thought you meant I was a klutz." I bit my bottom lip. "You weren't making fun of me?"

"Of course not. That's crazy," Todd said. "Everyone knows you're fast."

I thought about the cartoons and how I'd laughed at everyone else's. Maybe I'd been mad because this one was about me. "I guess it was pretty funny after all."

Todd looked at me and grinned. "Play soccer tomorrow at recess?"

"Sure."

Todd got up and went back to scribbling in his sketch pad. I smiled—I had my best friend back! But then I looked down at my messed-up macaroni pony and wanted to cry. What was I going to do now?

CHAPTER 9
The Pretty New Pony

"**I** heard something happened to your project," my mom said quietly when she came into Jessica's and my room that afternoon. When I had gotten home, I went straight upstairs and slammed the door. I had wanted to be by myself. But the sound of Mom's voice made me feel like talking.

"Yes." I played with my koala bear's ear and hugged him to me. "My picture was so good, Mom. I'll never make anything that good again."

"I'm sorry, honey." Mom stroked my back until I felt better. "Why don't you make a new one?"

"I used all the macaroni."

Mom stood up. "Well, I have another box downstairs."

"Really?"

"Sure," Mom said. "I was going to make it for dinner tomorrow night, but I think your project is much more important."

I smiled wider than I'd ever smiled before. "Thanks, Mom," I said, cheering up. I hugged her and ran down to the kitchen. Jessica was sitting at the table, digging in the cereal box for the prize. "Guess what, Jess? Mom has some more macaroni noodles. Want to help me color them?"

"Sure." Jessica grinned. "You can use some of my glitter too. You'll have the fanciest pony in school."

"And I'll guard this one so Caroline won't make another macaroni mess."

"Good plan," Jessica said. It was amazing how we thought alike sometimes.

My sister and I colored the noodles together. While they dried, I painted another pony. Then I glued on the macaroni.

"Here's the glitter," Jessica said.

I sprinkled gold glitter around the bridle and on the pony's mane and tail.

"It's beautiful!" Jessica gasped.

"It looks even prettier than a circus pony."

My heart was racing. Jessica was right. The day hadn't turned out so bad after all. This pony was even better than the first one!

When I went to school the next day, I couldn't wait for the show. Jessica and I wore our favorite new jumpers. Some of the boys got dressed up in nice shirts and pants. Lila was wearing a pretty pink dress that went perfectly with her magic wand. She looked like a fairy princess.

I was really excited about showing everyone my new macaroni pony. But I had to keep it hidden—I didn't want Caroline messing it up.

"Look." Lila frowned. "Todd's hanging up his mean pictures."

Some kids gathered around him as he hung them on the wall. Some of the kids were snickering, but Lila, Lois, and Caroline were still angry.

Todd had my picture in his hand. "If you don't want me to hang it—"

"Go ahead," I said. "My dad will get a kick out of it."

Todd laughed. "Get a kick—funny, Elizabeth."

I walked over to Lois, who was pouting. "Todd draws great cartoons, doesn't he?" I asked. "He drew my soccer feet."

Lois kept quiet.

"See, you like purple, so he drew you in purple," I said. "He knows that's your favorite color."

Lois smiled. Some of the other kids started joking about their own pictures, and pretty soon we were all laughing. Right before lunch I put my new macaroni pony right next to Todd's picture of me.

"I like it, Elizabeth," Todd said. "It's even better than the first one."

"Wow!" Ellen said. "It's so pretty."

Everyone lined up for lunch. But I wanted to hide inside and see if Caroline came back in to mess up my new pony. I slipped behind the closet door and hid. Everyone's feet pounded down the hall. The room grew quiet. I held my breath and peeked around the corner. The room was empty.

Then I heard footsteps. I slowly looked around the edge of the door. It was Caroline!

I was right. I held my breath again. My hands were shaking. She walked over to my pony picture and stared at it.

Then she reached out and touched the macaroni!

CHAPTER 10

Who Stole the Macaroni?

"Stop!" I jumped out from behind the closet.

"Yikes!" Caroline screamed. "What are you doing? You scared me to death."

I stepped toward her. "I was waiting to see if you'd come back in and tear up my pony again."

Caroline crossed her arms. "I was just looking at it. I told you I didn't tear it up."

"You were touching it!"

"I was thinking how pretty it was, but

I wasn't going to ruin it. I came in to work on my project." Caroline stepped on a paintbrush. The brush flew up into the air and came down right on my feet. I got green paint on my ankle socks!

Caroline's eyes grew wide. "I didn't mean to—"

I grabbed a brush with orange paint on it and flicked it at her. The paint splattered on her hand.

"Elizabeth!" Caroline picked up a brush with blue paint and flipped it at me. The paint went all over my arms. That did it! We both grabbed brushes and started a big paint fight.

"Hey!" Winston ran into the room with a painting in his hands. He put it aside and stepped between us, holding up his hands like a referee. But Caroline and I flipped brushes one more time. Paint soared through the air and landed on top of Winston's head, right in his hair. The orange paint made a big blob, then started running down his face. He looked up toward his hair as a streak dribbled down his cheek.

Suddenly Caroline started to laugh. Winston was making a silly face. I could tell he was really mad, but he looked goofy. I couldn't stop myself from giggling. Then Winston started laughing too. We were all covered in paint from head to toe!

We looked so funny that we began sticking our hands in the paint and putting handprints all over each other's clothes. Then I grabbed a whole bottle of green paint and dumped it over Winston's head!

"I've been slimed!" Winston cried, laughing.

Just then Mr. Crane walked in, leading the class. "What happened?" he asked, frowning.

Caroline clutched her stomach and giggled. "We're turning ourselves into paintings."

"Well, I hadn't planned on putting you guys in the art show," Mr. Crane said. He glanced at his watch. "And it won't be long until your parents get here. I want you to get cleaned up immediately."

Caroline and I nodded, and the three of us rushed to the bathrooms. I got the paint out of my hair and skin, but my dress had big wet colored blotches on it. It reminded me of one of Winston's paintings.

When we came back to the room, Winston's hair was dripping wet. Water drizzled down his cheek, and he still had a yellow spot on his nose. The rest of the classroom had been cleaned up by one of the janitors. Mr. Crane warned us never to have a paint fight again—and if we did, he'd call our parents. We promised we wouldn't.

Suddenly Jessica screamed. "Petey's loose!"

"Macaroni pony, macaroni pony," Petey squawked.

We all turned to see Petey flying across the room. He was sitting on one of the art display tables and flapping his wings.

"Macaroni pony, macaroni pony," Petey repeated. Then he turned around and pecked at my new macaroni pony! A noodle fell to the floor and made a clattering sound. Everyone gasped.

"Oh, no!" Eva cried. "He's eating your macaroni pony, Elizabeth."

I couldn't believe what I saw. Petey had a macaroni noodle in his beak and was hopping around like he was the happiest bird on earth. *He* had made the macaroni mess, not Caroline!

I moved Petey away from my picture. "Petey, I can't believe it was you," I said. I glanced up at Caroline and felt terrible. "I'm sorry, Caroline."

Caroline smiled. "It's OK."

"Petey want a noodle. Petey want a noodle," the parrot cawed.

The class burst out laughing.

"I shouldn't have blamed you, Caroline," I said.

"It's all right." Caroline studied her shoes. "I was pretty jealous of you. Your project looked so good." She went to her desk and took out her potato. "That's why I kept sneaking in here during recess. I was trying to fix my project. I let my mom help me with the other doll, but I felt bad. Everybody else in the class is making cool stuff of their own."

"I like the potato doll," I said. "I've never seen anything like it. And I would never have thought of it myself."

"Really?" Caroline's eyes widened.

"Really." I took the potato from her. I remembered the arms and legs and material Caroline had been using. "Do you still have your supplies?"

Caroline's forehead wrinkled. "Yeah, why?"

"Let's fix him." I sat the potato on the table. "If we hurry and work together, you can show it at the art show."

Caroline squealed in excitement. She took out her materials, and we made new arms and tied a piece of cloth around the potato for a dress.

"Let's use the little buttons for eyes," I said. "I think the others were too heavy. That's why they fell off."

"You're right," Caroline said. "And I'll stick toothpicks in the buttonholes to help them stay on till they dry."

"Perfect," I said.

Jessica and Lila watched us. "Good job," Jessica said.

Lila ran to her desk and came back carrying her art kit. "I think you should have this, Caroline. 'Cause your project is the most different."

Caroline clapped her hands to her face in surprise. "You think so?"

Jessica and I agreed. Caroline popped open the kit and found some red felt for the doll's mouth. She took a black pen and drew eyebrows above the button eyes.

When it was finished, Caroline hugged me. "It's fun working together."

"Much more fun than fighting," I said.

"Class, your parents are coming," Mr. Crane announced. "Everyone stand beside your project."

81

Everyone scrambled around the room. Mom and Dad came in and waved, and Jessica and I gave them twin smiles. My smile was so big, I thought my face would crack.

"Well, let's see your works of art," Dad said after he and Mom came over. They looked so happy and proud, I don't think they even noticed the paint on my clothes. But they were pretty used to seeing me get my clothes dirty anyway.

"You made a beautiful crown," Mom said to Jessica.

"That's right," Dad said, hugging Jessica. "It's just perfect for you, my little princess."

"And here's the famous macaroni pony," Mom said. "The glitter looks so beautiful in the light, Elizabeth."

Dad hugged me too. "I had no idea

my girls were such great artists!"

Mr. Crane came over and shook our parents' hands. "How do you like the show?"

"It's wonderful!" Mom clapped.

"Really great," Dad said. "Though you should keep an eye on Jessica. If she puts on that Cinderella crown she made, she could wind up turning into a pumpkin."

"Pumpkin . . ." Mr. Crane stroked his chin thoughtfully. "Thanks, Mr. Wakefield. You've just given me a great idea."

Is Sweet Valley Elementary about to go pumpkin crazy? Find out in Sweet Valley Kids #73, **THE WITCH IN THE PUMPKIN PATCH.**

Jessica's Macaroni Maze

Jessica wants to find some more macaroni noodles to give to Elizabeth. But she has to get through a big maze first! Grab a pencil and help her out! Can you get all the way through the maze without hitting any dead ends? Good luck!

Maze Answer

Elizabeth's Art Project

Elizabeth wants to paint other pictures, but she doesn't know what they should be. Can you draw something on her easels? Here are some ideas:

● Your favorite animal or pet

● Your family

● Your school

● Your best friend

● A flower

● A pretty design

Draw anything you want—
use your imagination!

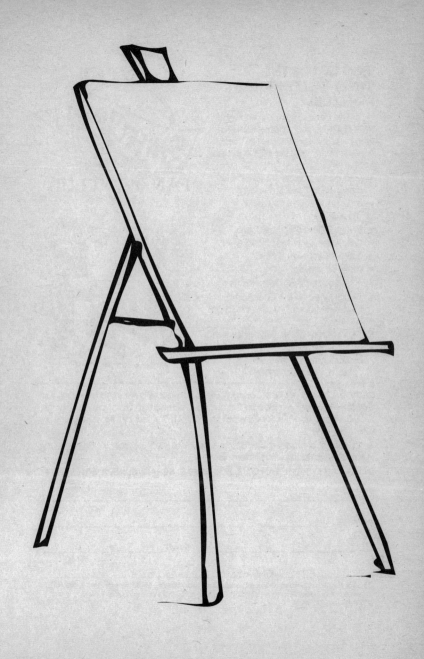

SIGN UP FOR THE
SWEET VALLEY HIGH®
FAN CLUB!

Hey, girls! Get all the gossip on Sweet
Valley High's® most popular teenagers
when you join our fantastic Fan Club!
As a member, you'll get all of this really
cool stuff:

- Membership Card with your own
  personal Fan Club ID number
- A Sweet Valley High® Secret
  Treasure Box
- Sweet Valley High® Stationery
- Official Fan Club Pencil (for secret
  note writing!)
- Three Bookmarks
- A "Members Only" Door Hanger
- Two Skeins of J. & P. Coats® Embroidery
  Floss with flower barrette instruction
  leaflet
- Two editions of *The Oracle* newsletter
- Plus exclusive Sweet Valley High®
  product offers, special savings,
  contests, and much more!

Be the first to find out what Jessica & Elizabeth Wakefield are up to by joining the
Sweet Valley High® Fan Club for the one-year membership fee of only $6.25 each
for U.S. residents, $8.25 for Canadian residents (U.S. currency). Includes shipping
& handling.

Send a check or money order (do not send cash) made payable to "Sweet Valley
High® Fan Club" along with this form to:

SWEET VALLEY HIGH® FAN CLUB, BOX 3919-B, SCHAUMBURG, IL 60168-3919

NAME _____
                        (Please print clearly)

ADDRESS _____

CITY_____ STATE _____ ZIP_____
                                                              (Required)

AGE _____ BIRTHDAY_____ /_____ /_____

Offer good while supplies last. Allow 6-8 weeks after check clearance for delivery. Addresses without ZIP
codes cannot be honored. Offer good in USA & Canada only. Void where prohibited by law.
©1993 by Francine Pascal   LCI-1383-123